Dear Parent:
Your child's love of reading starts here!

Every child learns to read in a different way and at his or her own speed. Some go back and forth between reading levels and read favorite books again and again. Others read through each level in order. You can help your young reader improve and become more confident by encouraging his or her own interests and abilities. From books your child reads with you to the first books he or she reads alone, there are I Can Read Books for every stage of reading:

SHARED READING
Basic language, word repetition, and whimsical illustrations, ideal for sharing with your emergent reader

BEGINNING READING
Short sentences, familiar words, and simple concepts for children eager to read on their own

READING WITH HELP
Engaging stories, longer sentences, and language play for developing readers

READING ALONE
Complex plots, challenging vocabulary, and high-interest topics for the independent reader

ADVANCED READING
Short paragraphs, chapters, and exciting themes for the perfect bridge to chapter books

I Can Read Books have introduced children to the joy of reading since 1957. Featuring award-winning authors and illustrators and a fabulous cast of beloved characters, I Can Read Books set the standard for beginning readers.

A lifetime of discovery begins with the magical words **"I Can Read!"**

Visit www.icanread.com for information
on enriching your child's reading experience.

Marley: The Dog Who Cried Woof Copyright © 2011 by John Grogan. All rights reserved. Manufactured in China. No part of this book may be used or reproduced in any manner whatsoever without written permission except in the case of brief quotations embodied in critical articles and reviews. For information address HarperCollins Children's Books, a division of HarperCollins Publishers, 10 East 53rd Street, New York, NY 10022.
www.icanread.com

Library of Congress catalog card number: 2011925977
ISBN 978-0-06-198944-5 (trade bdg.)—ISBN 978-0-06-198943-8 (pbk.)

11 12 13 14 15   SCP   10 9 8 7 6 5 4 3 2 1   ❖   First Edition

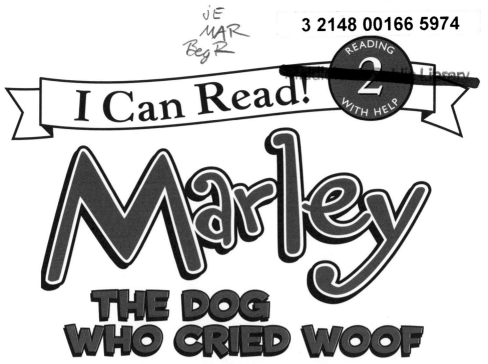

I Can Read!

READING
2
WITH HELP

Marley
THE DOG WHO CRIED WOOF

**BASED ON THE BESTSELLING BOOKS
BY JOHN GROGAN**

COVER ILLUSTRATION BY RICHARD COWDREY

TEXT BY SUSAN HILL

**INTERIOR ILLUSTRATIONS BY
LYDIA HALVERSON**

HARPER
An Imprint of HarperCollinsPublishers

Mommy was busy.

Daddy was busy.

Even Cassie was too busy
to play with Marley.

Marley heard a noise outside.

He ran to the door and barked.

"Woof! Woof!"

"What is it, Marley?" said Mommy.

Mommy looked out the door.

She saw a lady walking her dog.

"Woof! Woof!"

"Marley, be quiet!" said Mommy.

"It's just another dog."

Marley saw someone out the window.

"Woof! Woof! Woof!"

"Marley, what is it?" said Daddy.

Daddy looked out the window.

"It's only the mailman," Daddy said.

"Now be quiet, Marley.

I'm trying to write."

Marley poked his head
into Cassie's room.
He wanted to play.
"Not now, Marley," said Cassie.
"I'm painting a picture."

Marley heard something loud.

He jumped onto Cassie's lap

and barked.

"Woof! Woof!"

"Marley, what is it?" said Cassie.

Marley ran over to the window

and barked.

"Woof!"

Cassie looked out.

"It's only a garbage truck," Cassie said.

Mommy was busy cooking dinner.

Marley barked and barked and barked.

"Honestly, Marley, what is it now?"

Mommy said.

Just then a little boy rode by

on a tricycle.

Ting-a-ling!

He rang his little bell.

"Was that the big problem, Marley?"

Mommy asked.

"A tricycle?"

Mommy shook her head.

"Do you have to bark

at every little thing?"

Daddy was writing inside.

Marley was barking outside.

Daddy tried to ignore him.

But Marley didn't stop.

Daddy went outside.

Marley was chasing a squirrel

around and around a tree.

"I'm tired of you
barking at nothing,"
Daddy said.
"Woof," barked Marley.
"That's it!" yelled Daddy.
"If you bark again, I won't come!
I won't!"

Marley hung his head.

He didn't bark at nothing.

He barked at dogs!

He barked at the mailman!

He barked at trucks and bikes
and squirrels.

He didn't want his family
to miss anything!

Marley went to lie down

under a tree.

He didn't understand.

But he would try not to bark.

Baby Louie crawled out the door.

"Uh-oh!" thought Marley.

Baby Louie crawled toward the gate!

Marley knew he shouldn't bark.

He ran in front of Baby Louie.

He ran circles around him.

But Baby Louie did not stop.

Marley had to bark.

He just had to!

"Woof! Woof! Woof! Woof!
Woof!"

He barked as loud as he could.

Daddy came running.

"Marley!" Daddy yelled.

"For the last time, be quiet!"

Daddy saw Baby Louie crawling away.

He ran to scoop him up.

Daddy held Baby Louie close
and looked at Marley.

"You bark at every truck and trike.

You bark morning, noon, and night.

I've got only one thing

to say to you," said Daddy.

"Thank you, Marley," said Daddy.